STREETS OF GOLD

Rosemary Wells
pictures by Dan Andreasen

Dial Books for Young Readers *New York*

Based on Mary Antin's classic memoir,
The Promised Land

—

To Jacqueline Herchenroder,
1946–1996
Children's Librarian
—R.W.

For Al,
with many thanks
—D.A.

When she was twelve years old, Mary Antin and her family arrived in Boston, Massachusetts, after a five-thousand-mile voyage from Russia. The year was 1894, a time when the laws of Russia forced Jewish people to live in horrible conditions. The Antins considered themselves lucky to escape.

Several years later, in a long letter to relatives left behind, Mary Antin wrote an account of her family's suffering in Russia, their journey halfway around the world, and their experiences in America. When she became a young woman, Mary greatly enlarged upon her letter and it became *The Promised Land*, a several-hundred-page book that made her famous in her time.

I found an old copy on a back shelf of my town's library and was immediately drawn to Mary's story. I loved her courage, her passion for learning, and her enthusiasm for her adopted country. I was touched by the closeness of her family, which was the reason Mary survived and flourished. It was astonishing to me that a young girl who had lived in the United States for only six months could have written a thirty-five-stanza poem in English and published it in a Boston newspaper. But it is a true story.

Mary Antin wrote several different versions of *The Promised Land*. She herself changed names and details of her life from one account to another. Her book can be a difficult one to read, with an enormous gallery of characters. To bring it to today's young readers, I have culled and rearranged, shortened and simplified. Mary's own words, however, accompany each episode.

It is my hope that Mary Antin's story will live again for a whole new generation of American readers.

Long ago and far away in Russia my father held me in his arms. Together we looked out the window. Against the sky we saw the church dome in the shape of a huge onion, painted with real gold leaf. On every street were birch trees and oak timbered houses as dark as Turkish coffee.

"Look at the winter birches, Masha," my father said. "They are the color of your hair." And sure enough, their scarlet buds were exactly like my wild red hair.

"I was warm and watched over at home. . . ."

5

"My city and other places were grouped together as the 'Pale of Settlement,' and within this area the Czar commanded me to stay, with my father and mother and friends—because we were Jews."

My mother and father owned a little grocery store, and we lived upstairs. The store was in the Jewish section of town. Most Russians looked on Jews as an inferior and non-Russian race. All the same, many Russians chose to live alongside us. We were surrounded by them, but my family and other people of our religion lived very different lives.

Russians made rules and laws for Jewish people that stained the very air yellow. Our fathers were told what kind of work they could do, and they could do no other. Our brothers were stolen by the Czar's army while they were still little boys. Only short-nosed Jewish boys could attend school. The Czar's police came by with a ruler one day and measured my brother's nose. Joseph's nose was too long, and so Joseph could not go to school.

My big sister, Frieda, said the Russians were as dangerous as untrained animals.

Behind our grocery door hung a portrait of a hood-eyed man. He was Czar Alexander, ruler of all Russia.

"Why must we have his picture, Papa?" I asked.

My father answered, "When the Czar's soldiers come into the shop, they will not make so much trouble for us if they see the picture there."

I didn't dare walk in front of the Czar's portrait. I believed if I held an apple up to the Czar's painted eyes, they would slice through it as fast as razors.

At night the Czar ruled my dreams the way a constellation rules the icy sky. Many times I crept into my mother and father's bed.

My father said, "You are like a little warm duck egg beside me, Masha." At last I told him about the Czar's slicing eyes.

My father wrapped me up and took me downstairs by candlelight into the cold grocery store. He passed his hand in front of the Czar's painted eyes. Nothing happened. He lifted me and told me to touch the face and the eyes with my fingers. Nothing happened. He carried me back to bed and put me between himself and my mother so I would sleep without bad dreams. I was never again afraid of the Czar's picture.

"The Czar always got his dues, no matter if it ruined a family."

9

y mother taught me how to count using dried beans. Her fingers flew back and forth across the kitchen table, adding, taking away, until I got it right every time.

"One day, Masha," said my mother, "you must work in the shop and know how to count."

"Why can't I learn in school?" I asked.

"Because you are a girl and you are Jewish," said my mother. "Jewish girls are not allowed to go to school."

"Why not?" I asked tearfully.

Frieda gave me a warning look. We never spoke of this again.

But each afternoon I stood in the doorway of my father's store watching the Russian children, their hair wheat-blond, going home from school. The girls were dressed in neat brown pinafores and black aprons. The boys were in trim uniforms with many buttons. What I wanted was in those children's book satchels.

Frieda always called me away. Then she set me to ironing shirts or scouring pots. Frieda didn't mind that the rest of her life would be spent cleaning and ironing. The ache of that destiny used to come on me suddenly like a shove from a stranger.

"For a girl it was enough if she could read her prayers. After that she was done with books."

One Saturday at sunrise I lay in bed and listened to the sounds around me. I heard a voice echoing sadly up and down the crooked streets.

I woke my sister. "Who is that?" I asked Frieda.

"That's Blind David," Frieda told me. "Long ago when he was six years old, the Czar's soldiers kidnapped him. They made him a swill boy on a pig farm. He lived in the pigpen."

Blind David's cry was like a dove's calling for a lost mate.

Frieda went on. "After he lost both eyes in one of the wars, the army let him go. The poor old man can't even remember his mother's and father's names. He keeps hoping one of them is still alive and might know his voice. Papa gives Blind David bread and soup in the back of the shop late at night after you and Joseph are asleep."

So I listened for Blind David every Saturday morning. Hope hid in his voice and stripped my heart like beautiful music. Still, in those gray dawns I was glad to lie beside my sleeping sister with only David and me awake, and God, waiting for people's prayers.

"There were men whose faces made you old in a minute. They had served under Nicholas I. . . ."

In the summer my father sometimes rented a horse and cart. Together we went deep into the country-side to buy fresh herbs and chickens for the store. We trailed with us the smell of wood lavender and poppies we picked for Mother and Frieda.

The long midsummer days lasted until ten at night. With our horse's reins slack across his lap, Papa taught me to read and write from each of the five books we owned. Together we made up poems and recited them to the trees and birds. Over and over Papa told me how his mother had carried him to school through the snow in bare feet, so he would be an educated man. It was then I first heard the word America.

"They don't care what religion you are there," Papa said. "No Czars who give you bad dreams, no secret police who tell us where we can go or what we can't do."

"Where is America?" I asked him.

Father passed me a handful of wild strawberries and said America was thousands of miles across an ocean. I knew we could never make that trip.

"I read them hungrily, all the books there were—a mere handful, but to me an overwhelming treasure."

14

In October of that year the Czar's police closed our little grocery store. We had no idea why. Father was not allowed to do any other kind of work.

He and I went into the woods to pick mushrooms to sell on the street corner. We stood under the pines holding baskets full of honey mushrooms and chanterelles. Father reached into his pocket and brought out a gold ring with a cloud-blue stone. I had never seen anything so beautiful.

"It is a sapphire," Father explained. "It was given to me by a blind man just before he died. It is worth enough for my passage to America."

I turned the precious ring around in my fingers.

"We will starve," my father went on, "unless I cross the ocean and find work in America. I will send for you."

I could not speak, I missed him so already.

My father opened his black coat with the red silk lining and pulled me close to him. He smelled of pencils and licorice. I listened to his heart.

"My father was inspired by a vision. He saw something— he promised us something. It was America."

F ather left one Thursday morning after giving Mother the little money he had and promising to send more from America. We did not know whether he was alive or dead until his first letter arrived four months later.

Soon after, the Czar's police swooped down on us. They said we owed money, and all our possessions were to be taken away and sold. We didn't owe money, but no one would listen to us.

The police stamped through our hallways in huge squeaky leather boots, shaking the glass in the cabinets. They placed a yellow label saying PROPERTY OF THE STATE on everything we owned, every rickety chair and pair of shoes in our house.

I hid in a secret closet under the stair. I stood, wrapped inside the black coat my father had left behind to keep Mother warm. I felt its soft red lining between my fingers and listened to my father telling me not to be afraid. I breathed his licorice-pencilly smell, and I could hear him as clear as a bell from America.

"The fear of the moment was in my heart. . . . It was a horrid, oppressive fear."

We were able to rent a few small, dark rooms above a tea and coffee store where Mother found work for the two of us. Frieda cleaned house for a banker's family, and Joseph was a coal boy. For more than a year we saved every kopeck for our passage to America.

One winter night I delivered a kilo of coffee to a very grand house. My legs were white with sleet. The cook gave me a glass of steaming tea while she lined my broken shoes with newspaper.

I peered into the parlor. Green velvet chairs looked like shoulders of moss in the summer woods. Firelight danced on the spines of a hundred books. Before a writing desk was a girl my age.

"What do you want?" she asked me. I wanted her silky hair, her shoes. I wanted the world inside those books, but I couldn't say a word. The girl gave me a three-kopeck tip. I dashed home over the ice in my newspaper-lined shoes.

Every few weeks Father sent a little money for our passage to America. We hid it in the pocket of his black coat. But even better than the silver coins was a letter from America. "Masha, my little poet," the letter said, "there are free schools for every girl and boy here in America."

I ran my fingers over those words so many times, the ink blurred from the page.

"We had absolutely no reliable source of income, no settled home, no immediate prospects. But my mother made every effort within her power. . . ."

Finally there was enough money for the cheapest passage to America. Our journey to join Father began with a train.

The crowded railway station was the last I saw of my home. I watched from the train as our neighbors and relatives, come to see us off, became a blur of hands waving to us, throwing kisses and bits of paper with last words of advice. Among them were my sister, Frieda, and her new husband. I never saw them again.

The unheated train took us to Warsaw, through Prussia, to the docks in Hamburg, Germany. By the weak light of dawn, all the passengers were assembled in a high-walled brick building near the docks.

Chattering wardens flapped and fussed us into orderly lines. "'Raus! 'Raus!" they yelled. Flouncing in their white uniforms, they looked like a species of huge, German-speaking poultry. Our clothes were taken from us and boiled. We ourselves were sprayed with clouds of carbolic soap vapor and steaming water.

"Why are they doing this?" my mother cried.

"They say we are carrying terrible diseases," explained a passenger who understood German.

Until our boat sailed, we were kept under guard in a warehouse. At night I sometimes thought I could hear my father singing to me, songs only he and I knew because we had made them up.

"We emigrants were herded at the stations, packed in the cars, and driven from place to place like cattle."

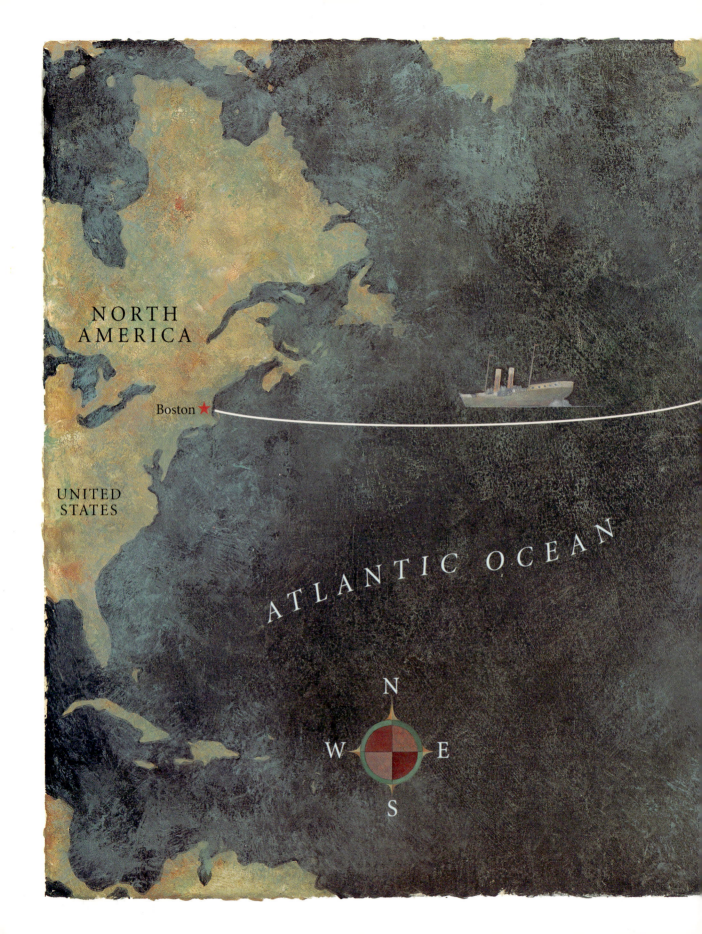

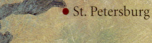

St. Petersburg

★ The start of
Mary's Journey

RUSSIA

● Hamburg

Warsaw ●

Berlin ●

GERMANY

EUROPE

AFRICA

MARY ANTIN'S JOURNEY
1894

· · · · · · · travel by train

——— travel by boat

We were many days at sea. Joseph and I stayed on deck away from hundreds of seasick passengers below. There we met a boy from Moscow who told us the streets in America were paved with gold bricks. We didn't believe him because if it were so, Father would have put this in his letters.

Our ship cut a deep wake through the surface of the ocean. Behind us the gray water shot into bright foam. Just underneath opened an inner curl of warm green that glowed like light in glass. The sea was as alive as the blood in my veins. I stared at it as if it were the face of a new friend.

On the seventeenth morning we saw distant bands of rock at the western edge of the sea. It was the port of Boston. "Land!" someone said, and then the whole shipful of people appeared at the rail, shouting, "America!" in one voice.

We waited all day to be inspected and to have our precious papers stamped at the Boston customs pier. At five o'clock, by the faraway bells of the Old North Church, we stepped into the sunlight. My father received us in his arms.

"I was conscious only of sea and sky. I felt as if I had found a friend, and knew that I loved the ocean. . . ."

Father took us by trolley to our new home on Dover Street. English words bounced through the Boston air. I could not read the street signs because the letters of the English alphabet were like nothing I had ever seen. Americans' faces seemed to me so different from wintery, waxy Russian faces. And the clothes Americans wore were so bright and funny, I had to close my eyes.

"What is the matter, Masha?" my father asked me.

"I am closing my eyes so I don't get dizzy," I told him.

In our apartment Father gave us a strange fruit called a banana that slipped out of its yellow wrapper. He showed us a chair set on two curved pieces of wood that allowed it to rock back and forth. He had bought cloth to make new dresses. It was in a curious pattern of crossed colored lines called plaid.

We walked through the cobblestone streets to the free public baths where we washed away weeks of sea salt. The streets were lit with hundreds of gaslights. Joseph said it was like the land of the wizards.

"America was bewilderingly strange, unimaginably complex, delightfully unexplored."

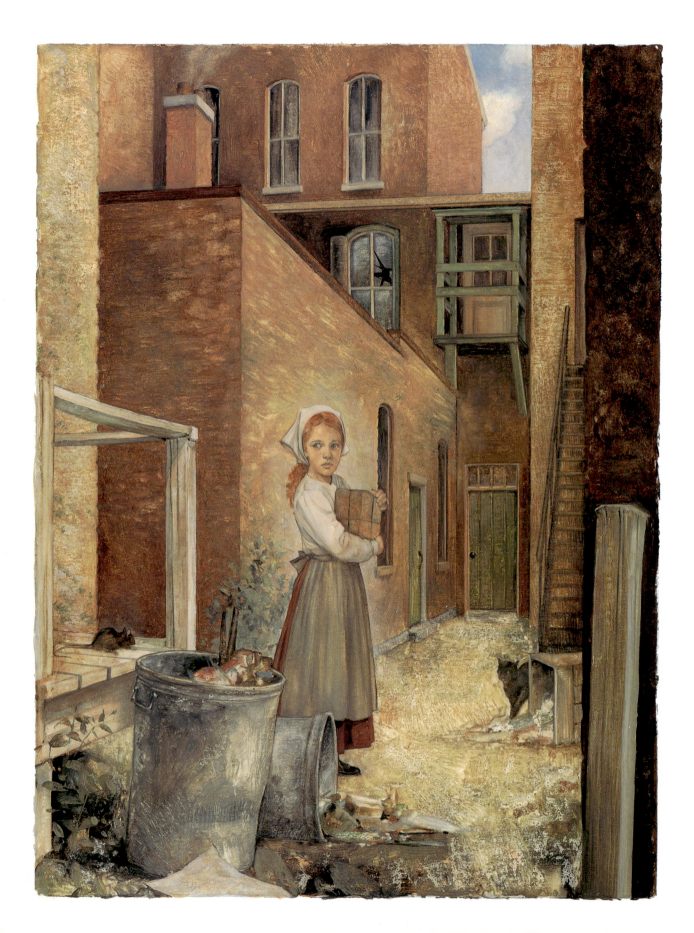

ot everything was fine and clean in this new land. Downstairs lived a man and a woman who fought all the time. The narrow stairway leading to our apartment reeked of smoke and burned fat. Dover Street was not paved with bricks of gold. Instead it was piled high with garbage that people threw out their windows. Drunks got themselves arrested, and Mother warned me about opium dens and thieves being on every street corner.

Our building was so hot and noisy, I had to escape to the roof. Tenement rooftops were a patchwork of melting tar and clotheslines. There I sat in the wind under the flapping laundry.

"So we came to Dover Street where rent was low. The ultimate cost of life, in terms of human happiness, was high enough."

In September Father took us to our first day of free American school. Mother braided my hair so tight, it hurt. I wore a dress she had sewn for me late into the night. Joseph had brand-new shoes that Father said cost a week's pay. We were put in the first grade.

I had just turned thirteen. My classmates were just beginning to lose their front teeth. To me they were like little chattery squirrels.

On that first morning in the classroom of South Street Grammar School, Father sat crammed into a child-sized desk beside my teacher. In his tongue-tied English he tried to explain to Miss Dillingham that Joseph and I would work hard to deserve what she was going to teach us. Miss Dillingham listened to Papa's impossible sentences.

In Russian Father said, "Miss Teacher, you have taken my children into the kingdom of heaven."

Miss Dillingham did not speak a word of Russian. But she met his eyes, and I knew she understood every syllable he said.

"It was with a heart full of longing and hope that my father led us to school on that first day."

My name was changed to an American name, Mary, so that I would fit in with everyone else. In six months' time I could speak English well enough to move to the fifth grade.

Father and Mother wanted me to tend the counter in the grocery store after school. When Americans and I spoke in English about the weather and the quality of the week's milk, my parents' eyes rested on me so proudly, I felt as if feathered birds had lighted on my shoulders.

"The principal asked me to write a poem about George Washington," I said to my father in early June of my first school year.

"Who is George Washington?" asked my father.

I replied, "He was the Father of America. He never told a lie, and he made everything free, including school for girls."

"Like a good czar," said my father.

"No," I said. "Not like any kind of czar at all."

"The name I wished to celebrate was the most difficult of all. Nothing but 'Washington' rhymed with 'Washington.'"

"I dug the words out of my heart, squeezed the rhymes out of my brain, forced the missing syllables out of their hiding-places in the dictionary."

was asked to read my poem in front of the whole school on graduation day. And so I did, my voice quavering.

Later Miss Dillingham, my first teacher in America, stopped me in the hall.

"Your poem is good enough to be printed in the newspaper, Mary," said Miss Dillingham.

So after school she took me and my poem across Boston by trolley to Hanover Street, where the newspaper buildings were.

The Boston Herald printed my poem, all thirty-five verses of it. That night I imagined my verses lying on hundreds of kitchen tables and arms of chairs all over the city of Boston.

A NEWCOMER'S TRIBUTE
TO FREEDOM

by MARY ANTIN

'T was he who e'er will be our pride,
Immortal Washington.
Who always did in truth confide,
We hail our Washington!

(CONTINUED ON TENTH PAGE)

Before sunrise I heard the jingling bottles that announced the milkman. I could not sleep. On our roof the early morning air was cool. I sat against a chimney and wrote a letter to my sister.

I struggled with the words. How could I explain to her? In the alleyways were thieves and dope addicts, and I had to walk among them. But on the grassy Boston Common people laughed aloud and wore clothes that were all the colors of the rainbow. I was thirteen years old and had had a poem printed in the newspaper! In my old language I tried to explain to Frieda that you had to be an American to understand these mysteries.

I watched the mist lighten over North Boston. The building tops were massed like palace walls with turrets and spires lost in the dawn clouds. The sun hung just above the edge of the sky. I saw its light shoot over the wet cobblestones and for one moment the streets turned to gold.

I loved my city and my place in the world. Then I used my new language, English, and I spoke to the sunrise, "I'm on my way," I said, "here in America!"

"In the pearl-misty morning, in the ruby-red evening, I was empress of all I surveyed from the roof of the tenement house."

Published by Dial Books for Young Readers
A member of Penguin Putnam Inc.
375 Hudson Street
New York, New York 10014
Text copyright © 1999 by Rosemary Wells
Pictures copyright © 1999 by Dan Andreasen
Designed by Karen Robbins
Printed in Hong Kong on acid-free paper
First Edition
1 3 5 7 9 10 8 6 4 2

Library of Congress Cataloging in Publication Data
Wells, Rosemary.
Streets of gold/by Rosemary Wells; pictures by Dan Andreasen.—1st ed.
p. cm.
Based on Mary Antin's classic memoir, The promised land.
Summary: Based on a memoir written in the early twentieth century,
tells the story of a young girl and her life in Russia, her travels
to America, and her subsequent life in the United States.
ISBN 0-8037-2149-8
1. Antin, Mary, 1881–1949—Juvenile literature.   2. Jews—United
States—Biography—Juvenile literature.   3. Jews—Belarus—Polotzk—
Biography—Juvenile literature.   4. Immigrants—United States—Biography—
Juvenile literature.   [1. Antin, Mary, 1881–1949.   2. Jews—
United States—Biography.   3. Jews—Soviet Union—Biography.
4. Immigrants—United States.]   I. Andreasen, Dan, ill.
II. Antin, Mary, 1881–1949.   Promised land.   III. Title.
E184.J5W467   1999
973'.04924'092—dc21   [B] 97-50377   CIP   AC

The art was rendered in oil on gessoed board.